MW00882493

PEN♥PAL®
Gals

To my daughters, Reese & Hailey

Your beautiful, sweet souls inspire me each day.
May your passion for life inspire others.

Love
xoxo

www.mascotbooks.com

Pen Pal Gals: Friends Forever

©2022 Julie Thiessen. All Rights Reserved. No part of this publication may be reproduced, stored in a retrieval system or transmitted in any form by any means electronic, mechanical, or photocopying, recording or otherwise without the permission of the author.

Second printing. This Mascot Books edition printed in 2022.

For more information, please contact:
Mascot Books
620 Herndon Parkway #320
Herndon, VA 20170
info@mascotbooks.com

Library of Congress Control Number: 2021908691

CPSIA Code: PRV0921B
ISBN-13: 978-1-64543-524-2

Printed in the United States

PEN♥PAL®
Gals

Friends → Forever

By Julie Thiessen

Illustrated by Vanessa Alexandre
and Julie Thiessen

CHAPTER ONE

The Trip to Camp Lake Shore

"School is out for summer!"

Reese and her classroom friends jumped up and down with joy. The sun was out, the weather was hot, and their work was complete. Reese loved school, academics, art, and reading, but now she was excited to seek new adventures outside.

As she grabbed her backpack and ran out the door, she had just one thing on her mind—the vacation at Lake Shore Retreat, her favorite place in the whole world.

Reese and her family spent most summer weekends at the camp enjoying swimming, boating, tubing, biking, and eating delicious campfire food. The first week of summer was always a special trip, as the family spent every moment together under the big trees by the beautiful lake, relaxing and celebrating the beginning of summer. She could not wait to boat around the lake while sitting on the large tube with the cool wind in her hair and warm sun on her shoulders. It sounded scary, but it wasn't—half the fun was falling off!

As soon as she got home from school, Reese traded her backpack for her favorite bag: a bright-pink striped duffel bag with a dolphin patch sewn on the front. She stuffed as much as she possibly could into it. Clothes, of course . . . a bathing suit . . . hiking boots . . . and then some of the fun stuff, including books, paper, markers, and her music player with headphones. Barely able to zip up the bag, she set her pillow alongside her sleeping bag as her mom called up the stairs.

"Reese! Are you ready?"

She jumped up and grabbed her things, racing to the car. Reese's mom smiled at her before buckling her baby sister into the car seat next to her brother. Dad was nearly finished packing up the car, but Reese noticed something was still missing.

"Dad, don't forget the big tube!" said Reese as she climbed into her seat with her plush pillow in her arms.

Finally, her mom shut the car door and off they went. Looking out the window with anticipation made Reese feel like it was a long car ride, but she knew they were only an hour away from their campout adventure. They had been coming to Lake Shore

Retreat as a family for years, so she knew the whole route by heart. She counted each landmark on the path with excitement from the moment they left their neighborhood.

The sun was already setting when they arrived at the entrance of the camp. It got much darker at night underneath the big canopy of oak trees. Through the fading daylight, many families were entering their own campsites, setting up tents and building fires to cook their dinners. Laughter filled the air; everyone was happy to come to Lake Shore Retreat!

Reese and her family pulled up to their campsite and tumbled out of the car. They set up the huge tent and pulled out their supplies—sleeping bags, clothes, and cooking gear. She loved to camp and spend the very first week of each summer here with her family.

Even though it was getting pretty late, they were all eager to walk down and visit the most beautiful spot in the whole camp— the big, calm lake. Together, they admired how the water's color faded from blue to black. There were just a few boats still on the water as the sun finally sank entirely into the horizon and the sky filled with the brightest stars and moon ever seen.

Tired from the long day of school, work, and driving, they walked back to camp to settle in for the night. After everyone had crawled into their tent together, Reese lay on her pillow, listening to the crickets and unique sounds of the nighttime forest and dreaming of the days ahead. Every summer at the lake was full of outdoor adventures, but she just knew that something unique and special was about to happen.

CHAPTER TWO

A Special Camp Friend

Reese was the first to wake up the next morning, excited to start the day and visit the lake. She crawled out of the tent to enjoy the cool morning air and the sounds of all the birds singing.

Pretty soon, her whole family was awake and walking around. They made breakfast together and enjoyed eating around the small campfire, which Dad built, while they all talked about the things they wanted to do first.

"I think I'll go for a walk to check things out!" Dad said.

"I want to come, too!" Reese's brother shouted happily. "Then, can we go out on the boat?"

"I want to go swimming first," Reese said.

"That's wonderful," Mom added. "Your sister and I will come down to the lake with you to splash around."

They enjoyed the walk together, stopping every few moments to examine an interesting plant or point out a pretty bird or funny squirrel. As they walked on the path to the lake, Reese could peek through the trees to all the campsites along the way. She marveled at how quickly they had filled with small tents and families, and enjoyed the sounds of all the people waking up and getting ready to start their days. She wondered what types of adventures each one would have and thought about how much fun it would be to have a friend at camp to enjoy her own summer adventures with.

"Reese, look!" Mom said in a whisper as they walked into a particularly bright, sunny spot between the trees. "Look around us!"

Reese stopped suddenly and couldn't believe her eyes. There were dozens of butterflies dancing around them, going from flower to flower and enjoying the sunshine.

"Wow!" Reese whispered, not wanting to scare them away. "I can't believe how lucky we are to see so many of them this close!"

Mom laughed. "I know! How much more lucky can we get than to be here by the lake on such a beautiful day?"

Reese smiled at her mom. "Yes, I guess that's true . . ."

"Is something bothering you?" Mom asked.

"No! This is my favorite place in the whole world!" Reese exclaimed. "I'm very happy to be here. I just kind of wish I had a friend to share all of it with."

"Well, maybe next weekend you can invite a friend to come along with us," Mom offered.

Reese paused in her tracks and scrunched her eyes shut tight before wishing aloud for the special friendship she wanted. The moment she opened her eyes, she heard a sweet, soft voice in the distance. "Mom, let's go!" the voice said. "Summer is here and Lake Shore Retreat is waiting for us. I think I want to swim first!"

Reese's heart started to beat faster as she realized the voice she'd heard had sounded like a girl around her age. Somehow, she just knew this was her wish coming true, but where was this voice coming from?

Skipping through the forest with her mom and sister close behind, Reese could finally see the beautiful blue lake ahead. Next to it was a small gathering of tents, including a bright pink one that matched the color of Reese's favorite duffel bag. A ray of sun gleamed right onto this pink tent, illuminating a girl with soft blonde hair just like hers.

Reese watched in awe as the girl jumped off the dock and into the water without a moment of hesitation.

"Mom, can I go swim now, too?" Reese asked.

"Of course," her mom said. "Have fun!"

Unlike the other girl, Reese waded slowly into the water, enjoying the difference between the warm morning air and the cool water. Once she'd dipped her head in, though, Reese was ready to go, and she quickly swam over to meet her new friend.

"Hello," said Reese. "You're a really amazing swimmer. You look just like a dolphin in the water!"

"Thanks!" the girl said proudly. "Dolphins are my favorite animal!"

"Really?" Reese said, surprised and happy. "Dolphins are my favorite, too! My name is Reese; what's yours?"

"My name is Addie."

The two girls smiled at each other, both knowing a friendship had already formed. They began to talk about all of their favorite activities and found that they shared so many: drawing, ballet, music, and swimming were just a few.

After they had exhausted themselves playing in the water, Addie came up with a new idea.

"Do you want to listen to music with me?"

asked Addie.

"Yes, of course!" said Reese as they swam back to shore and ran over to her mom and sister.

"Mom, this is my new friend!" said Reese happily. "She loves dolphins, dance class, and drawing just as much as I do!"

Reese's mom smiled at the girls. "And you look like you could be twins!"

Addie smiled at Reese's mom. "Hello, my name is Addie! May Reese come over to my campsite so we can listen to music?"

Impressed by Addie's manners, Mom replied, "Hello, Addie, it's very nice to meet you. I would be happy to walk over with you two to meet your mom and make sure she approves."

Addie and Reese skipped together arm-in-arm toward Addie's campsite with Reese's mom and sister just a few steps

behind. Addie's mom was there when they arrived, relaxing and setting up camp. The girls quickly got permission to listen to music together, and they crawled into the small pink tent and shared songs they loved back and forth while the adults talked. They were happy to discover that they even shared the same favorite song.

After a little while, Reese and Addie were both hungry for lunch and ready for the next adventure, so they went to find their families. Everyone had gathered together close to the water.

"There you are!" Reese's dad said, wrapping his daughter in a hug. "I thought I was seeing double there for a second!"

Both families marveled at how much Addie and Reese resembled each other, then shared the plans they had been making with the girls.

"How do you two feel about us all making up some lunch and taking it out on the boat as a picnic to share?" Reese's mom asked.

Both girls clapped and started talking about the boat ride, the huge inflatable tube, and more swimming.

It really was the perfect day. They spent hours jumping on and off the boat, enjoying snacks, and riding around on the tube as the boat led them around the lake so fast the whole shore seemed to fly by. The first time Addie fell off the tube, she got water up her nose and started to sputter, but she was laughing so hard that everyone knew she was alright. After that, both girls enjoyed falling off the tube many more times.

By the time the sun started to set again, everyone was tired and maybe a little sunburnt. They were each ready for warm, quiet dinners and early bedtimes. The girls hugged each other, already looking forward to the plans they had made for the next day.

"Goodnight, Reese," said Addie.

"Goodnight, Addie, see you tomorrow," Reese said, waving behind her as she left.

As they walked back to camp through the darkening forest, Reese smiled as she passed through the trees where the butterflies had fluttered. Although all the butterflies were gone now, her wish had come true. She was excited to spend the rest of the summer week getting to know her new friend, Addie.

CHAPTER THREE

Camping Adventures

The two girls were inseparable as they explored the camp together over the following week. They exchanged their favorite books, listened to every new song, and colored pictures for one another to hang up in their tents. They loved to write each other notes, hiding them in their sleeping bags for each other to find. Reese taught Addie how to make paper flowers, and Addie taught Reese how to draw a butterfly perfectly. They hiked through the woods and

made up wonderful stories to share with each other. They practiced the ballet movements they had both learned in dance class. They swam every day, and Addie taught Reese a few tricks about diving she'd learned in swim class. As long as they were together, whether they were making meals over the campfire or jumping off the dock into the cool water of the lake, they felt a sense of closeness. It was almost as if they were sisters. Reese and Addie had become best friends.

The week raced by in a series of the best and most fun days Addie and Reese had ever had. As the sun set over camp once again, they settled into their new nightly routine.

"It's time for s'mores, everyone," said Addie's mom.

They were glowing with complete satisfaction as they carefully roasted their marshmallows over the open campfire. Reese preferred her marshmallows a light golden brown, but quickly realized that Addie liked to set hers on fire and enjoy it charred on the outside. They laughed together over their different tastes as each indulged in graham cracker sandwiches filled with gooey marshmallow and chocolate. It was the perfect way to end another beautiful summer day.

The warm camp was now dark. Stars filled the night sky, and there was a quietness that surrounded the two girls. Reese could hear the nighttime animals scurrying and the buzzing bugs over the crackle of the logs as the campfire died down. Reese and Addie both sat and thought about how they would be returning home the next morning.

"I am going to miss you, Reese," said Addie as she gazed at the glow of the fire,

watching the bark melt away from a log.

"I'm going to miss you, too!" Reese replied. "But when we come back next weekend, we'll have all sorts of new things to share with each other. I'll bring my special ribbon and some beads so we can make friendship bracelets, and you should bring that book you were telling me about . . ."

Addie looked at her, surprised, then shook her head. "No, Reese, my family doesn't come back here every weekend like yours does. We live hours away and only come to Lake Shore Retreat for one week every summer."

Reese's heart sank. She'd felt sad to leave her friend for only a week, but for a whole year? That seemed impossible!

Addie saw the look on Reese's face, and she reached over to hug her. "Oh, Reese, I'm sorry! I thought you knew! I'll miss you very much, but I promise to see you again next summer."

"But what if you forget about me? What if I forget about you?" Reese asked, her eyes welling up with tears. Addie was her best friend, her special camp friend, but what would happen once they weren't spending every day together?

"I'll never forget about you!" Addie said fiercely. "We are best friends forever. You should take the drawing I made you and put it up in your room when you get home to remind you of all the fun times we've shared. I will make you another drawing, too."

Reese liked the idea of having more of Addie's drawings, but did not want the fun times to end. Reese wanted to continue to hear all about Addie's school, books, music, and dance class, and she wanted to continue to share the things she loved with Addie.

They still had so much to share with each other, and she knew they would miss each other terribly.

As Reese gazed into the bright orange glow of the fire, she became determined to find a way to stay connected to her new best friend.

CHAPTER FOUR

Goodbye Forever?

"Roll up your sleeping bag nice and tight," said Reese's dad as he packed the car, trying to figure out how he'd managed to get everything in there in the first place.

"But, Mom," Reese said, ignoring her family breaking down camp all around her, "can't we just go pick Addie up next weekend? Then she can come back to camp with us!"

Reese's mom shook her head. "I'm sorry, Reese. I know you'll miss your friend, but she lives very far away. Why, it would take us almost all day to drive down and pick her up. Plus, Addie's mom has told me about all the other things they are doing this summer. Addie has a big ballet recital coming up, she has swim meets, and they'll be visiting family all over the country. She will be having other adventures, just like you."

Reese clutched the note she'd written to Addie late the night before and the beautiful drawing she'd made of the two of them swimming together. She'd stayed up to make the letter perfect, working late until her parents had needed to tell her to turn her flashlight off and go to sleep. She was sad that her brilliant plan to see her friend again wasn't going to work.

"I need to go find Addie and say goodbye," Reese said.

Reese's dad checked his watch. "Okay, but

you better hurry. We need to hit the road very soon, and I'm sure Addie's family is getting all packed up, too. You can run over to their campsite, but turn right back around if they are already gone."

Reese's heart skipped a beat. She hadn't even considered that her friend could already be gone! What if she never had the chance to say goodbye?

She raced through the woods, keeping her eyes peeled for her best friend's bright pink tent. It wasn't until she stood in the very middle of their vacant, empty campsite, clean and all packed up, that she realized she was too late.

Reese turned sadly and walked back down the path through the woods toward her own family's campsite, holding the note and the drawing she'd made for Addie in her hands. Her eyes began to fill with tears once more, and they were just about to spill out when she turned a corner and saw the sunny patch that filled with dancing butterflies each morning. Standing right in the middle of the ray of sunshine was Addie! Her curly blonde hair, big smile, and sun-kissed face glowed so brightly.

Reese ran over and threw her arms around her. The two girls laughed and almost tripped over one another.

"I thought you had already left!" Reese said.

"I wouldn't leave without saying goodbye!" Addie cried out. "When my family pulled up to your campsite, your dad told me you'd already left for ours, so I ran straight over without even thinking about it! I had to give you this," she said, shyly handing Reese a folded sheet of paper. "I wrote you a long note last night to thank

you for being my best friend."

Reese gave her a huge hug and handed over the note and the drawing she'd made for her. "I was so worried that I would never be able to give this to you. If I'd had to keep this drawing at home for a whole year, it would have gotten lost or misplaced or my brother and baby sister would have found it and made a mess of it."

Addie unfolded the drawing and smiled happily. "Reese, this looks just like us! I can feel the water right through the page." Her smiled turned upside down as she added, "Trading notes and drawings with you has been one of my favorite things about this whole week. I'm going to miss everything about our camp adventures, but I think I'm going to miss this most of all."

The flash of inspiration that sparked in Reese's head at that moment was even brighter than the sun bouncing off their matching golden curls.

"Follow me!" Reese shouted, grabbing Addie's hand and racing through the trees back toward her family's campsite.

CHAPTER FIVE

Pen Pal Gals

The two girls ran together, hand-in-hand, and arrived at the campsite in record time. Everything was all packed up, and their families were standing together, exchanging their own final goodbyes.

A brilliant idea had popped into Reese's head, and her mom was the first to notice the huge grin across her face.

"Mom, do we have any envelopes . . . and stamps?" asked Reese.

She knew that her mom loved writing

letters and always seemed to have some tucked away in her wallet. Her mom nodded as she rummaged through her bag and pulled out a few envelopes with stamps on them and handed them to her daughter.

Reese pulled her favorite pen from her backpack and carefully printed her own name and address on the first envelope, just the way her mom had taught her. She handed a blank envelope and her favorite feather pen to Addie.

"Would you please write down your name and address on this one, just like mine?" Reese requested.

Without questioning her, Addie filled the front of the envelope with her own information, looking back at Reese's example several times.

When she finished, Reese held out the envelope with her own information on it,

offering it to Addie. "Now, let's trade. We can be pen pals!"

Addie looked confused, but she was excited by her friend's excitement, her wide smile, and her laughter. "What's a pen pal?"

"Pen pals are friends who send letters back and forth to keep in touch—my mom taught me about them. She loves writing letters to her friends all over the world. She has an address book with all of their information stowed inside, and she's got boxes of letters they have written back to her! Now, we can write letters back and forth—that way, you can still tell me about your ballet and swim lessons and every adventure you get into this summer, and I can send you messages and pictures from right here at Lake Shore Retreat."

Addie was very happy with this idea; sending a letter to her friend and getting one in return sounded like fun.

"We can be Pen Pal Gals!" Reese exclaimed, as if they had just created a new kind of friendship pact for themselves.

"I'll write to you, and you can write back to me!" Addie promised. She clutched the envelope to her heart, and Reese knew that she would be hearing from her very soon. "Goodbye, Reese, it has been a fun summer vacation, and I can't wait to hear all about the rest of your summer. Don't forget to tell me everything!"

"You got it!" Reese said. "I can't wait to write you."

Two hearts were filled with joy, knowing their friendship would last and that they could still share so much of their lives with each other. They now had a way to keep in touch and spread the magic of giving each other gifts and sharing stories and secrets long after they left the campground. The girls hugged each other tightly, knowing that they'd just forged a pact that would make their summer adventure everlasting. Although they had to say goodbye in person for right now, the friendship had just begun.

CHAPTER SIX

An Everlasting Friendship

Reese had been home for a week and busy with other summer activities, but the thought of receiving a letter from Addie kept crossing her mind.

"Hi Mom! Has the mail come yet?" Reese asked.

Reese's mom smiled at her daughter and her excitement. "Yes," she said, "and another letter came from Addie."

She wondered if Reese and Addie's letters would continue to flow back and forth, and they did, all summer long. Throughout the whole summer, the two girls' commitment to being Pen Pal Gals only got stronger.

Becoming Pen Pal Gals was the perfect way for Addie and Reese to write to each other and continue their friendship. Though they were not able to spend the remainder of their summer vacations together at Lake Shore Retreat, the constant stream of letters, drawings, and gifts connected them. They shared more with each other through the course of the next few months than they ever imagined.

Even though they lived in the same state, they were hours apart, and the areas they lived in were very different. Although there were hundreds of miles between them, they knew their friendship would only deepen and grow as long as they were Pen Pal Gals.

Reese was able to tell Addie about the farm animals, nature, and wide-open skies. In exchange, Addie told Reese about her trips to the beach and splashing in the waves. Reese couldn't believe it when Addie wrote to tell her she'd seen a dolphin swimming in the crashing waves! Addie was equally excited to hear about the rides at the fair that came through Reese's town at the end of the summer, and the girls started to plan a visit for next summer, so they could ride the Ferris wheel and Sidewinder together. They loved sharing details about their homes and learning more about what daily life was like through each other's eyes. Together, the two girls shared a special friendship unlike any other they'd had before.

Both Addie and Reese were busy and involved in many summer activities, including hanging out with their friends,

dance classes, and birthday parties, but they did not forget about one another as they prepared letters and gifts to mail. Addie wrapped up a bright-red and white summer shirt she had bought for Reese, along with a few books she had already read and wanted to pass on. Meanwhile, Reese was designing a pink beaded bracelet complete with a dolphin charm to mail to Addie. The two girls had just as much joy in their hearts to send a Pen Pal Gals letter as they did to receive one from each other.

No matter what else she was busy with, Addie made sure to send an envelope that arrived each Friday before Reese's family left to go back to Lake Shore Retreat. Reese saved all the letters she received from Addie in a special oversized envelope pouch she had made with her mom. She wrote back to Addie at the end of each weekend about what new adventures she'd had at camp, the discoveries she'd made, and the things she was excited to share. Letter by letter, they carefully planned for the next summer.

Sharing their thoughts, dreams, and all of the things they were thinking about with each other created a unique and special Pen Pal Gals friendship. As the summer went on, they both learned they loved acting, and they shared their plans to be in plays and try out for different sports once the school year began again. The overwhelming excitement of waiting for the next letter to arrive was joyfully exhausting. Reese and Addie had become friends forever.

Reese created an address book where she copied Addie's address down from the original envelope with her favorite feather pen. Her mother admired the beautiful pink address book Reese had created. It became one of her most valued possessions, and she slowly filled it with the names and addresses of all her friends—but Addie's name would always come first.

As the summer came to an end, Reese realized the new kind of long-distance friendship she had created with Addie was her most cherished part of it all.

"It is really cool how Addie became part of my whole summer and my whole life when we've never even seen each other outside Lake Shore Retreat," Reese marveled. "I feel like the possibilities are endless between us!"

Her mom smiled and agreed. "Some things are just meant to be," she exclaimed.

CHAPTER SEVEN

Summer's End

On the very last day of the summer, Reese sat on the dock at the lake with her paper, pens, markers, and stickers. She began writing and watching her whole family enjoy the beautiful end of their vacation. Splashing around in the cool lake water with the warm sunshine on their shoulders was the perfect end to their summer.

Reese's family had invited many friends out to the lake on the weekends, and Reese, of course, had invited her friends to enjoy swimming and boating, too. They had saved the very last weekend of summer for just their family to enjoy each other. They were ending the summer just as it had begun, celebrating the best season of the whole year and their favorite place in the world together.

As Reese wrote her letter, she tried to capture every last detail of this moment, hoping that Addie would be able to experience it just as clearly. They had enjoyed their campfire meal and taken their last boat ride; the giant inflatable tube had been dried off and had all the air taken out, ready to be stored away for the next few months.

Although Reese missed seeing Addie, their Pen Pal Gals friendship was a special friendship: a long-distance forever friendship.

Of course, Addie and Reese would

continue to write each other letters long after school started again—for years and years, in fact. Reese had designed her own brightly colored Pen Pal Gals stationery and sketched pictures of her favorite things. She smiled as she looked down at the ballerinas, dolphins, and hearts that decorated the pages, knowing how excited Addie would be to share these with her. She'd even written a special message at the top of the paper—"Write me and I'll write you back!"

Walking back to the campsite, Reese stopped at the clearing between the trees where she'd first wished for a special camp friend. She remembered hearing Addie's voice ring out, and the way her hair had glowed in the bright sunlight. It really was the perfect summer. Reese had received so much more than she could have imagined with Addie's friendship. She could not wait to mail out the letter on her new stationery and receive one back in the mail from Addie. In fact, Reese had created several Pen Pal Gals with many of her special girlfriends, grandparents, and cousins. She received several letters a week and loved responding to each one.

Thinking about what a special summer it had been, Reese finished her letter to Addie and tucked it into the pink envelope that matched the color of her favorite bag and Addie's tent. She decorated it with stickers and drew a special heart with wings next to her name. Dropping her letters into the outgoing mail always brought a huge smile to her face. Reese loved becoming Pen Pal Gals with all of her friends, and she couldn't wait to see what adventures, stories, and friendships the brand-new year would bring.

Write me and I will write you back!

PEN♡PAL®
Gals
→ *girlfriends*

xoxo

A Letter for you

PEN♥PAL® Gals

Love

Write me and I will write you back!

PEN♥PAL®
Gals
➤➤➤⟶ *girlfriends*

Things I like ...

xoxo

sending
sweet *notes*

Gals

PEN♥PAL®
Gals

About the Author

Julie Thiessen has always had a passion for creativity, design, and adventure. She enjoys spending time with her family boating around the lake, fishing, skiing, hiking, and exploring new places. She is a business owner, graphic designer, and busy mom of three. Her daughter, Reese, was the inspiration behind Pen Pal Gals when she began writing letters to her friends to stay in touch. Julie values her own lifelong friendships and wanted to inspire other children to write letters and stay connected when they have to be apart from friends and loved ones. Julie lives along the Central Coast of California with her husband, two daughters and son.

PEN♥PAL®
Gals